Mister TOOTS

Emma Chichester Clark

HarperCollins *Children's Books*

One wild, stormy day, Bella opened her front door and found a little stranger on her doorstep.

"Goodness!" she said. "You'd better come in before you get blown away!" The little creature shivered and followed her into the kitchen.

"Have a glass of water," said Bella. The little creature was **terribly** thirsty.

"Would you like some cornflakes and broccoli?" asked Bella. The little creature was **dreadfully** hungry too.

"Do you feel better now?" asked Bella. The little creature just **stared** up at her.

"You don't understand a word I'm saying, do you?" said Bella.

Just then, Tulip and Tadpole rushed in.

"Oh! Mummy!" cried Tadpole. "What is he? Can we keep him?"

"Well, I think he's lost," said Bella,
"and I don't think he speaks our language."

"Toot! Toot!"
cried the little creature, and waved his arms.

Bella, Tulip and
Tadpole took him up
and down every street
in town and asked
everyone if they knew
the little creature.

But nobody did.
No one had ever
seen him before.

"Poor little thing . . . all on his own," everyone said.

By the end of the day, Bella, Tulip and Tadpole still didn't know where the little creature had come from, but the little creature had learned to say "hello" and "goodbye" and "thank you".

When they got home, the little creature climbed on a chair and stared out of the window at the sky.

At bedtime, Tulip and Tadpole made him a comfy bed and kissed him goodnight.

But in the morning he was back
at the window **again**.

Tulip and Tadpole did everything they could to distract him and cheer the little creature up . . .

and after a while . . .

he began to join in.

He learned to play lots of different games with Tulip
and Tadpole over the next day or two . . .

. . . but sometimes he looked **so sad,**
and he still often stared up at the sky.

"It's as if he's looking for someone
or something," said Tulip.

They wondered and worried about the little creature.
"We don't even know his name," sighed Tadpole.

"Let's call him **Mr Toots!**" said Bella.
"Because toot toot was the first thing he said to us."

Mr Toots beamed at Bella.

"He likes it!" said Tulip.

They **loved** him with all their hearts.

Everybody did.

The neighbours popped in to see him all the time . . .

and helped him settle in.

All the cousins and uncles and aunts **adored** him.

"He's the **sweetest** thing!"
said Aunt Esther.

"I **wish** we could take him home with **us**!" said
Rupert and Clarence.

"I **wish** he was **mine**!"
said Aunt Jemima.

But one day a terrible thing happened . . .

They went to the big park where there were lots of tall trees.

"Toot! Toot!"
cried Mr Toots,
and he began to run.

Toot! Toot!

"Wait!" cried Tulip.
"Wait!" cried Tadpole.

But Mr Toots kept on running.

Bella watched with alarm . . .

. . . as he disappeared between the trees.

"Come on!" she cried.
"He can't have gone far!"

When they caught up with him,
he was standing under a large
chestnut tree. There was something
hanging from the branches.

"Mine!" said Mr Toots.

Mine!

"I didn't know he knew that word," said Tulip.

"What is that thing?"
asked Tadpole.

"It looks like a basket,"
said Bella.

Mr Toots jumped up and
started tugging at it.

Tulip grabbed his ankles and
Tadpole grabbed Tulip and Bella
hung on to Tadpole, and they
all pulled together.

CRASH!

The basket suddenly came free.

Then, just as suddenly,
the wind picked up and
the basket began to fly away.

And Mr Toots jumped inside it!

WHOOSH!

"MR TOOTS!" cried Bella.

But the basket and Mr Toots were whooshed away in the wind.

Bella, Tulip and Tadpole ran as
fast as they could, but they were
TOO LATE . . .

Mr Toots was sailing,

up and up . . .

over the treetops.

He was soon far out of sight.

"MUM!" wailed Tulip.

"MUM!" cried Tadpole.

"Oh, my darlings!" said Bella. "I think our little Toots may be going back to where he came from."

Mr Toots!

"I thought he'd stay with us **forever**," said Tulip.

"I thought he **loved us**," said Tadpole.

At suppertime, none of them felt like eating.

At bedtime, Tulip said . . .
"I miss him **so much**
already."

"How can I sleep when I
don't know where he is?"
asked Tadpole.

Bella didn't sleep a wink either.

When friends and neighbours heard that Mr Toots
was missing they came to comfort them.

"Maybe he's happy where he's gone," said one.
"Perhaps you should try to forget him," said another.

And the days went by.

Soon it was a whole week
since Mr Toots had gone.

"I think he's **definitely**
forgotten us by now,"
said Tulip.

"We're **never** going
to see Mr Toots again,
are we?" said Tadpole.

Bella didn't know how to answer them.

Just then, there was a knock at the door . . .

. . . and there was
Mr Toots!

He grabbed Tadpole's paws.

"He wants us to follow him!" cried Tadpole.

"Come on, Mum!" cried Tulip. "Run!"

And as they ran they were joined by others . . .

More and more. Soon, the whole town was following Mr Toots.

Then, suddenly, everyone stopped.

They could **hardly believe their eyes.**

The sky was filled with baskets . . .

And the sound of little toots.

As the baskets landed, all the
little creatures jumped out of them
and ran towards the waiting crowd.

They were all given a warm welcome.

There was
someone for
everyone.

It **didn't matter** that they didn't speak the same language, because they all understood each other **perfectly.**

"So where would you like to go now, Mr Toots?" asked Bella.
"HOME!" said Toots.

"Forever?" whispered Tulip.

"Forever!" said Tadpole.

"And EVER!"
cried Mr Toots.